W9-BMT-630

DISCARD

GROTESQUE

by Scott R. Welvaert

www.12StoryLibrary.com

12-Story Library is an imprint of Peterson Publishing Company and Press Room Editions.

Produced for 12-Story Library by Red Line Editorial

Photographs ©: makosh/iStockphoto, cover (background), 3 (background); Viacheslav Lopatin/Shuttersock Images, cover (foreground), 3 (foreground)

Cover Design: Laura Polzin

ISBN
978-1-63235-163-0 (hardcover)
978-1-63235-202-6 (paperback)
978-1-62143-254-8 (hosted ebook)

Library of Congress Control Number: 2015934307

Printed in the United States of America
Mankato, MN
June, 2015

CHAPTER
1

Sunset. Brooklyn, New York.

A siren wailed in the distance. A delivery truck lumbered down the street. The aromas of tomato and basil drifted down the street from Tony's Ristorante Italiano. People entered their houses and apartment buildings after a long day of work. Some neighborhood children wrapped up their stickball game and retreated indoors.

Raine crouched on the ledge of St. Genevieve's bell tower and took in the last of the sun's rays. The lower the sun fell, the faster his body thawed. His muscles and ligaments loosened. His heart thumped faster in his chest. With each passing minute, his hardened exterior softened. His wings shook off the stony petrification. His tail, too. His bared claws and fangs retracted. His skin rippled with life. As the last sliver of sun dipped below the horizon, he blinked his dry eyes. Raine took in a great breath and stood on creaky, achy legs. He had been a grotesque for nearly three hundred years. A few aches and pains were to be expected.

Raine stifled a yawn and then entered the bell tower. Inside was his room. He found his clothes: a pair of baggy jeans, a long-sleeved shirt, high-top sneakers, and a gray hoodie. Looking into a dirty mirror leaning up against the wall, he thought he could pass as human—as long as no one looked too closely.

Around him, the bell tower held the mementos of his years at the church: newspaper clippings, his journals, a small statuette of Lady Liberty, a stuffed bear from Coney Island, charcoal sketches of people taking a night stroll in Central Park, and an easel with a half-finished watercolor of the Brooklyn Bridge at night.

For most of his life Raine lived at St. Genevieve's. During the day, as a grotesque, he sat petrified, perched high above the church grounds. At night, as flesh and blood, he was free to help the pastor with the church. He repaired the crumbling masonry, rotting wood railings, and broken windows. They even had an old-fashioned push mower to keep the crabgrass down on the grounds—as strange as it was to cut the grass in the evening. This church was his bond to the human world.

Once a cathedral in France, St. Genevieve's had been struck by a bomb during World War II and nearly destroyed. But a wealthy American salvaged what he could and moved each surviving stone, Raine included, to Brooklyn. Raine still missed his original home, its people, the food, and the simplicity of life. He missed the crushed amber tones of Pas-de-Calais, France. The bustle of wooden carts. The bells. The gentle flow of the fountain in the courtyard. Life would never be that good again, he thought. But it could be worse.

Raine heard voices downstairs. Pastor Ramón Hernandez was meeting with the church board.

"I'm sorry," one man said. Owen Larson. The head of the board. "There's nothing more we can do. The bank will foreclose. We have to sell the church."

6

"We can still work on increasing the size of the congregation," Pastor Hernandez said.

"Ramón," said an older woman. Probably Margaret Woodward, one of the longtime board members, Raine thought from the sound of her voice. "You've done all you can. We've been putting this off for far too long."

"But—" the pastor began.

"We're sorry, Ramón," the woman said, cutting him off.

When the board walked out, Raine climbed down from the bell tower and into the pantry, which opened up into a small kitchen. But the pastor was nowhere to be found. Raine checked his office. Nothing. Finally, Raine went to the sanctuary and found Pastor Hernandez sitting alone in the front pew, his head bowed and his hands together in prayer. A full moon shone through the stained-glass windows, bathing him in moonlit colors.

Without looking at the grotesque, the pastor said, "Raine, you don't need to wear that hood around me."

Raine lifted his hands and pushed the hood back.

"After three hundred years, it's kind of a habit," he said.

The pastor handed Raine an old leather journal stuffed with yellowed, tattered pages. "And you left this in the annex last night. Might be wise to keep a better eye on it."

"Sorry." Raine wanted to ask about the meeting, but felt afraid to. He wrung his leathery hands together in worry, and then said, "Another visit from the board. Any good news?"

Pastor Hernandez took a deep breath and sighed. "No. Numbers are still down, and they won't increase the budget. We just don't have a large enough congregation to support the church anymore."

"If they sell, the new owners won't tear down the church, will they? I mean, if that happens, then I—"

Pastor Hernandez looked up at Raine with sadness in his eyes. "I know," he said. "I know how important it is for you."

"My fate is tied to this building," Raine said.

Pastor Hernandez stood and rubbed his head. "Yes. Yes. The three rules: *Stone by day, flesh and blood by night. Each grotesque is bound to its building's plight. One life to give, to make it right.* But yours won't be the only life affected."

"I know," Raine said, more to the floor than to the pastor. But the pastor was right. There was a greater battle at hand. The church helped so many other people in this poor neighborhood.

The pastor collected his thoughts and said, "If there is one thing I believe in, it's that there is always a way to make people see. To see the good that we provide the community. Hopefully something will remind them of that. We just need to give it more time."

More time, Raine thought. Nearly three hundred years old, and he still hadn't learned patience. "I don't know. I think we need to do something."

Pastor Hernandez stepped up to Raine and wrapped an arm around his shoulders. "Well, there's still work to do here. We need to prep for tomorrow's spaghetti dinner."

CHAPTER
2

All night Sunday, Raine cleaned the church and prepared for the spaghetti dinner on Monday night. He vacuumed the annex. Swept out the sanctuary. Cleaned the windows.

Then, Monday night, he woke and climbed down to the small kitchen in the church's basement. Large cooking pots full of spaghetti boiled on the stovetop. Pastor Hernandez wore an apron and worked on the sauce. He lifted a spoon to his lips and tasted it. "Hmmm. It needs something."

Raine stepped in and drained a large pot of pasta while the pastor added some fresh herbs to the sauce.

"So it's only us tonight?" Raine asked, knowing the answer. At every Sunday service, Pastor Hernandez asked for volunteers to help with the spaghetti dinners. Few answered his call.

The pastor nodded.

Just then a voice called out from the cafeteria. "Hello? Pastor Hernandez?"

"In the kitchen!" the pastor called back.

He took off his apron and hung it up. Then he washed his hands quickly and dialed the kitchen dimmer switch to a lower light.

"I'll leave, Pastor," Raine said.

"No," the pastor said. "You're fine."

Through the doors came two men. One Raine knew from before: Owen Larson, the head of the church board and a retired owner of the local grocery. The other man he didn't know. He wore a suit and tie, and he was sharply groomed. His shiny wristwatch looked as though it cost more than the entire church.

Owen stepped forward and shook the pastor's hand. "Pastor Hernandez, this is Joseph

Waldermann. He's placed the highest bid and will be taking over the property soon."

The pastor stepped forward and shook Waldermann's hand. "Welcome. It's nice to meet you."

Waldermann finished the handshake and pointed around the kitchen. "A bit dark for cooking, don't you think?"

"Saving on electricity," the pastor said and smiled. "We're preparing our spaghetti dinner."

Raine did his best to blend into the background. To be invisible. But as Waldermann looked around, he saw Raine. He stepped forward and extended his hand. "Joseph Waldermann."

Raine looked at the pastor, unsure of what to do. The pastor nodded, so Raine reached out and shook Waldermann's hand.

Waldermann retracted his hand quickly. He peered closely at Raine, trying to see the face hidden by the hood. "Interesting handshake. Who are you?"

Pastor Hernandez stepped over and said, "This is Raine. He's a steward of the church— our caretaker."

"His hand," Waldermann said. "It's rough . . ."

"He has a condition, sir," the pastor said. "And the church doesn't turn anyone away."

Waldermann took out a handkerchief and wiped his hand. Again, he laughed uneasily. "It isn't catching, is it?"

"No," the pastor said. "He's just . . . different." He paused, trying to change the tone of the conversation. "Mr. Waldermann, would you like a tour? To see the church?"

"No. That won't be necessary," Waldermann said. "I'm just interested in the lot. The church will be torn down."

Raine gasped. His heart lurched in his chest. Within him, an old anger raged. He was compelled to protect the church. His life depended on it. Reflexively, he unsheathed the claws in his leathery fingertips, but then folded his arms across his chest to hide them. He had to calm down.

Pastor Hernandez reached out and patted Raine's shoulder. The friendly touch calmed him. Soothed him.

"That sounds a bit rash," the pastor said. "Every community needs a church. It's the heart and soul of a neighborhood, Mr. Waldermann."

Waldermann let out a little laugh. "If that were true, then I wouldn't be here. Right?"

The pastor looked defeated. All he could do was sigh loudly.

"All right, then," Waldermann said, looking at his watch. "Thank you for your time."

With the conversation ended, Owen and Waldermann left.

This is all happening too fast, Raine thought.

Later, when they opened the cafeteria doors for the feast, a long line of people waited outside. The spaghetti dinners had started out as a fundraiser for the church. But few donations were received. The folks who came were mostly the neighborhood's hungry and needy. Pastor Hernandez greeted each one with a hearty handshake. He never turned anyone away.

"Welcome," he said. "Come in. Eat."

Raine stood behind a table, serving. As much as he wanted to fly straight out of the church and track down Waldermann, he knew that wouldn't end well. The pastor was right. Patience. They needed time to figure things out.

An elderly woman in rags and missing a few teeth held her plate up to him. Her hands shook terribly. Raine served her. Her eyes lingered on his hooded face as she withdrew and went to sit down. Next a man stepped forward in a dingy coat and stocking cap. His beard was matted. Raine served him, but the man didn't move along right away. He gazed over his plate and into Raine's face, hidden beneath his hood.

"You don't look so good," the man said.

Raine tried to smile. He tugged the hood over his head a little farther.

The man glanced around, as if wondering whether others saw the same thing he did.

"I have a . . . condition," Raine whispered.

The man squinted at Raine, then shook his head and turned away.

As the man walked away to find a place to sit, Raine looked up and noticed that Pastor

Hernandez had been watching the whole exchange. The pastor stepped in place next to Raine.

"You handled that well," he said as he served another guest.

"Freaks always trump the homeless," Raine said with a fake chuckle.

A couple of hours later, the guests had all been served. As Raine began tearing down the food line, a teenage girl stepped carefully through the doorway. She wore a yellow floral print dress and a yellow headband. Her wavy red hair fell to her shoulders. But what caught Raine's attention were her eyes. Pale blue. Almost the color of ice. He couldn't help but stare.

Once inside, the girl took a shaky step forward. That's when Raine noticed the white cane she held in one hand. The pastor quickly went to greet her. As he led the girl to the food line, they talked.

Before Raine knew it, this beautiful girl was standing right in front of him.

"This is Sophie," the pastor said. "She recently moved in across the street with her mother."

Again, Raine just stared at her. He didn't know what to say, and even if he had, he couldn't have gotten the words out. He nervously bit his lip and felt his face grow strangely warm.

"Hi," Sophie said with a smile.

"I'm so sorry," he finally managed.

Sophie stared back at him, through him, past him.

"Sorry for what?" she asked.

Raine fumbled over his words. "I was sort of staring at you."

Sophie smiled. A little laugh escaped her lips.

"Well, if you didn't notice," she said, "I stare all the time. If someone gets squirrely, I usually tell them they're really, *really* interesting. That's usually when they notice I'm blind."

Raine laughed. "Are you hungry?"

She shook her head. "Oh, no. I had come to volunteer, but Pastor Hernandez said I was too late."

"A little," Raine said. "I'm just starting to put things away."

"Raine," the pastor said, "You could show Sophie around the church."

"But you're the pastor," Raine said. "Shouldn't you give her the tour?"

The pastor smiled. Then he leaned closer to Raine's ear and said, "And don't *you* want to?"

"I'm pretty sure she can still hear you," Raine told him.

Sophie blushed and turned away.

The pastor gently pushed Raine away from the serving table. "I guess you have no choice now."

Reluctantly, Raine stepped around the table. "Hi," he said to Sophie.

"Hi."

"It seems weird to give you a tour," Raine said.

Sophie grabbed his arm and said, "Blindness doesn't make you enjoy what's around you any less."

"Right, okay." Raine fidgeted as he walked with her. He led her upstairs and to a set of doors.

"These lead to the sanctuary. It isn't too big, but it's—"

"So, is Raine your real name?" Sophie asked, cutting him off.

"Yeah," he said. "Though I spell it with an 'e' at the end."

"It's unique. I don't think I know anyone else with that name."

"My mother was an artist in France," Raine explained. "She said there was nothing quite like how the rain fell on the old buildings. How the water poured from the grotesques on the cathedral."

"Grotesques?"

"You know, like gargoyles," Raine said. "Many grotesques are used to channel rainwater off a building's roof. Some have other purposes."

"I never knew they were called that," Sophie said.

They continued to talk as they walked through the sanctuary.

"St. Genevieve's used to be a huge cathedral in France," Raine explained. "After World War II, much of it was salvaged and brought here—to build this church. It's smaller, but it still has the heart and soul of the original. My mother liked painting it."

"Fascinating." Sophie said. "Your mother sounds like a real free spirit."

Raine watched Sophie as she ran her hand along the carved wood moldings of the altar. He was so engaged in how she interacted with the world around her that he forgot she had spoken.

"So what's she like?" Sophie asked.

"Oh yeah, my mother was a free spirit. She really was."

"Does she have a studio here in the city, then?" Sophie asked.

Raine stopped walking for a moment. "No. She died years ago."

GROTESQUE

It had been many years since he had seen his mother, but he still remembered her face, her voice, and the way she perched on top of the cathedral during the day. A grotesque like him, she had taken Raine in as an orphan and raised him as her own. She had cared for him when he fell ill. He had been unconscious for days during the worst of his illness. When he awoke, Raine was fully healed, and she was dead. The Great Plague of Marseille had taken so many, but not him. Before his mother had passed away, she transferred her life force to him. Her grotesque gift healed him. Made him what he was. That had been in the year 1720. He had been without her for nearly three hundred years. Raine tried to smile.

"Let me show you more of the church," he said, hoping she wouldn't ask any more questions about his long-dead mother.

For the next hour, Raine showed her every nook and cranny of the church. And as he described everything, she ran her hands over the pipe organ, the stained glass windows, and the ladder leading up to the bell tower—"seeing" by feeling.

And she told him about herself. Raine listened. He smiled. He laughed. She said her favorite color was yellow. She loved Puerto Rican food. Old movies. Classic novels. Poetry. School. Her father was some bigwig banker or something. Her mother ran a nonprofit to help inner-city youth. Her parents had just gotten divorced. Her mom hadn't asked for anything except custody of Sophie. Sophie loved both her parents dearly, but she felt more connected to her mother.

Raine could relate.

CHAPTER
3

It's not that Raine didn't like sunrises. He did. He just couldn't experience them like normal people. While the city woke and came to life, he sat frozen in place. He could hear the birds chirping and see the day brighten. He saw neighbors leaving their homes in suits and dresses. They kissed their children, loaded with backpacks for the school day ahead. A couple holding hands ducked into the bagel shop. Maybe they'd sit and have a conversation over a cup of coffee before catching the bus to work. But he'd never experienced any of that. From his perch on the church ledge, high above the street, he saw and heard everything that went on around him. He just couldn't take part in it. He had to experience it from a distance. That was the curse of being a grotesque.

The morning after the spaghetti dinner, Raine crouched, frozen in stone. As he watched the activity on the street below, an eagerness filled him. For the past three hundred years, he had allowed himself to drift off to sleep immediately after sunrise. But this morning, he couldn't fall asleep. He wondered when he'd see her again. Sophie. A splash of yellow in this grey world. A vibrating hum rippled through his stone body as he waited. And it only stopped when he saw her emerge from the modest apartment building across the street.

She walked carefully down the steps and turned right at the sidewalk. Her cane tapped in a steady rhythm like a clock. Deep down, he hoped she would stop and look up at him on the top ledge of the bell tower. But he knew she wouldn't. She had no idea he was there. She had no idea what or who he really was. Frozen, he watched her until she left his field of vision. Until that sliver of yellow headband disappeared in the distance. Only then did Raine feel at ease and allow himself to sleep.

25

GROTESQUE

Most days, Raine dreamed of his mother. In his dreams, he was back in France in the cathedral's courtyard. He would be sitting on a hillside while his mother sat at her easel, painting. But a different dream invaded his resting mind today. A dream in which Sophie sat next to him on the ledge of the church. He was no longer a grotesque, and she had her eyesight. Both of them sat on the edge with their legs dangling. On the horizon, they watched the sun rise. They watched as it exploded into the sky with brilliant yellows, roses, and oranges.

Sophie cried at the beautiful sight.

And Raine sipped coffee.

It was the best and most vivid dream he could recall having. He could almost taste the coffee. Feel the warmth of the sun.

But it was all interrupted by a wailing siren. A whistling from above. An air raid. Around them, bombs exploded. Buildings toppled. Debris tumbled down. Raine reached for Sophie, but she was gone. The church was gone. The whole city of New York had vanished.

He was back at the cathedral in France during World War II. The wall beneath him crumbled, and he fell. He found himself buried beneath a pile of stone. Then everything went to black. As real as it felt, he knew it was just a dream, or rather, a nightmare. One he needed to wake up from.

When his eyes opened, Raine saw the sun had set. He was back in New York, on his ledge at the church. Everything seemed as it should be. But as he turned to stretch his stiff neck, Raine saw it. A wrecking ball. While he had slept, someone had parked a crane next to the church. And its large wrecking ball blocked his view of Sophie's apartment building.

Raine hurried into the bell tower and pulled on his clothes. An ancient anger flared up inside him, and his heart beat faster. His claws extended. He raced outside to the church grounds. His chest heaved in huge breaths as he approached the crane. With a rage he rarely unleashed, he leaped high into the air and with one quick slash from his claws cut the cable to the wrecking ball. It fell with a thud onto the ground.

That act of vandalism helped calm his rage. He stopped to catch his breath. And in the silence, he heard a shout down the block. He knew that voice. It was Sophie's.

Raine ripped off his hoodie and unfurled his wings. With quick, powerful thrusts of his wings, he launched himself up to the bell tower, where he crouched and scanned the neighborhood, listening. He heard Sophie's shout again—coming from an alley behind the grocery store. Raine dropped from the tower and soared over the streets. From above the alley, he saw two local troublemakers, Matt and Tommy. They were pushing and shoving Sophie into a corner as she cursed at them.

Matt and Tommy always fleeced the newcomers in the neighborhood. Sophie tried holding her own. She swatted at them with her cane. But that wouldn't stop them for long.

Out of the night sky, Raine shot down toward the thugs. He landed with a thump between the two teens. When they turned, he snarled and lifted them off the ground by their necks. Tommy's eyes were wide with fear. Matt screamed in horror. They clawed at Raine's face and arms, to no avail.

"Leave, now!" Raine growled.

Then he threw them up against the wall. He stood over them as they got back to their feet and ran.

"Raine?" Sophie asked.

Raine folded his wings behind his back. Even though she was blind, he felt as though she could see him.

"Sorry," he said softly.

Sophie stepped closer. "Sorry? Sorry for what?"

"I should have warned you," Raine said. "Matt and Tommy prey on all the newcomers to the neighborhood."

"Don't be sorry!" she laughed. "I'm glad you showed up. I'm good with my cane, but I'm no daredevil."

The closer she came, the more nervous Raine got. He shouldn't have taken off his hoodie. Soon, she was next to him. The yellow headband. The red hair. Those pale blue eyes.

He no longer felt afraid or nervous. He felt warm, as though she'd brought the sunlight with her.

"Are you okay?" she asked.

She reached out for his arm.

Raine pulled away. He didn't want her to feel his rough, leathery skin, or worse—the folded wings on his back. He didn't want her to know what he really was.

"What's wrong, Raine? They didn't hurt you, did they?" she asked.

"It's nothing," Raine said. Nervous again, he stepped away from her. Raine folded his arms across his chest. He wasn't cold, but he felt . . . exposed.

"I have to go."

"Wait a second! Where are you going?"

But Raine opened his wings and flew up and over the streetlights. Sophie's hair fluttered in his wake. Raine soared over the buildings. His wings stroked the air. He closed his eyes and flew, his wings outstretched, gliding. Feeling the wind currents ripple over his back relaxed him.

But even as he enjoyed the sensation of flight, he was stabbed by the feeling that everything felt like it was going wrong. The church. Mr. Waldermann. Sophie. The wrecking ball. He was beginning to believe it was his destiny to be destroyed with the church. To be reduced to a pile of crumbled stone.

He circled the church a couple of times in the night. When his heart stopped racing, he swooped around the bell tower. On his second pass, he saw someone sitting on the ledge of the bell tower. He adjusted course and landed.

"I'd give anything to fly like that," Pastor Hernandez said.

Raine sat down next to the pastor, and they both dangled their legs from the ledge— just as Raine had imagined in his dream, only with the pastor instead of Sophie. From the pastor's slurred speech, Raine figured he'd been there for a while. Probably tired and emotionally exhausted.

"My condition has its perks," Raine said. "And curses."

The pastor smiled. "I know."

"So were you waiting for me?"

The pastor nodded as he looked at the crane in front of them.

"You know they'll just reattach the wrecking ball, right?"

Raine nodded. "Yeah, I know. But I couldn't stop myself. I just woke up and saw it there, and . . . something snapped."

"You have to be careful of the attention you attract. The last thing we want is for someone to start investigating random acts of violence in the neighborhood," the pastor said.

"Yeah, I know."

After a moment, the pastor said, "I thought we really had a chance to save the church. I really did."

"As you always say, don't lose hope. Give it time."

"Oh," the pastor said, surprised. "You've got other ideas?"

"Maybe."

"Where'd you go just now, anyway?" the pastor asked. "I heard you whoosh off in a hurry."

"It was Tommy and Matt," Raine explained.

"Again? I thought I might have been getting through to them," Pastor Hernandez sighed. "You didn't hurt them, did you?"

"No. Mostly frightened them."

"What were they up to this time?"

"They were harassing Sophie."

"And she's okay?" the pastor asked.

"Yeah," Raine said.

"Good. She's a sweet, kind girl," the pastor said as he stood up. "Now I think it's best I get some sleep."

After saying goodnight to the pastor, Raine went about some random tasks to take his mind off things. He swept and mopped the floors. He polished the woodwork. He went outside to trim the roses in the garden.

When he ran out of chores, he climbed back up to his room in the bell tower to work

on his sketches. He had made hundreds
and hundreds of different drawings of St.
Genevieve's. But tonight, he found it difficult to
focus. He was worried about the future of the
church and kept thinking that there had to be a
way to save his home.

CHAPTER
4

All day, Raine sat motionless on his perch, his eyes staring ahead in stony sleep. He'd hoped to stay awake to catch a glimpse of Sophie again, but he'd fallen asleep. When the sun set, he awoke and stretched the stiffness from his limbs.

Stifling a yawn, he wandered into his room atop the bell tower. He found a new hoodie and got dressed. But as he looked about his room, he noticed something was missing. *Where were his sketches?* Normally, his room was filled with them—he kept them tacked to the walls and piled on the shelves. Each drawing was unique. Last night he had thought he might be able to sell them to make some money and help save the church. But now they were gone.

Raine climbed down the ladder to the pantry and walked through the kitchen into the cafeteria, calling out, "Pastor, have you seen my—"

But before he could finish, he saw Sophie and the pastor sitting across from each other at a large table. On the table were a stack of his drawings.

"Hello, Raine," the pastor said. "Sophie stopped by a little bit ago to talk, but I didn't want to wake you from your nap."

Sophie stood up and faced Raine. "After what happened last night, I wanted to make sure you were okay. I was surprised to find you were sleeping, but Pastor Hernandez told me about your aversion to light."

"Right," Raine said. "Sorry about that. I sleep during the day."

"Quit being sorry," Sophie said. "It's fine. I mean, it's not like you're a vampire or anything."

Raine took a step back, nervous. Sophie didn't realize how close she had come to guessing his secret. That he *was* a monster.

"So what are you doing with my drawings?" Raine asked. "I thought maybe I could sell them, for the church."

Sophie sat down carefully. "Pastor Hernandez told me about your artwork. These drawings are amazing, Raine. We thought maybe we'd use some of them to make flyers announcing the last church service."

Raine held up his hand and said, "Wait a minute. You like my drawings? How— How did you see them?"

"Sit here next to me," Sophie said.

When he did, Sophie found his hand and placed it on one of the drawings. Gently she pressed his fingers against the paper.

"When you sketch or paint, you always leave tactile impressions. They're faint, but they're there," she explained. "And those impressions are enough for me to picture what you were drawing."

Raine tried to feel the drawing with his fingertips, but couldn't feel anything.

"Are your eyes open?" Sophie asked.

"Yeah."

"Well, close them, silly. Your eyes take over otherwise. They don't let the rest of your body see anything."

Raine closed his eyes. The longer his eyes were closed, the more he was able to pay attention to the slight indentations the pencil had created on the paper. He was sure his fingers couldn't "see" as well as hers did, but he could feel the church unfolding under his fingertips. When he smiled, so did she. He wondered if she had been able to sense him smiling somehow.

Raine suddenly realized that she'd had her hand resting on top of his the whole time. His rough, leathery skin had been against the soft underside of her wrist. He fought the urge to yank his hand away. He'd been afraid his skin would disgust her, but it didn't. She didn't pull away.

"My hand," Raine said. "It doesn't freak you out? I mean, I know it's, well, different."

"I'm different, too. Does the fact that I can't see freak you out?" she asked.

"No."

"Then, we're square."

Pastor Hernandez cleared his throat. "Well, you two should get going. It's Friday night, and a lot of people will be out and about. We need to get the word out that the church is in imminent danger. If we can get everyone to come together for one last service, maybe a miracle will happen. Maybe if we all raise our voices in protest, we can stop this. It's not much, but it's something."

Raine and Sophie gathered up all the flyers and stuffed them into Sophie's satchel. Then they made their way out of the church. For more than two hours they walked around the neighborhood and handed out the flyers to everyone they met. Raine was just happy to have Sophie by his side. He enjoyed the enthusiasm in her voice as she talked to people about St. Genevieve's, and the sweet smile she flashed as she handed each person a flyer. Even at night, Sophie's face shone bright and happy. They stopped in at Tony's Ristorante Italiano and gave Mama Angelo a flyer. Sophie even gave the flyers out to people standing at the bus stop. The Johnson boys smiled from their stoop when she handed them one. Pedestrians, beat cops, taxi drivers.

She stopped them all and made her best pitch to support the church. A few people recognized her from helping out with her other charities. Everyone they met seemed charmed by Sophie.

He wondered what the people thought, seeing this radiant girl walking next to the hooded freak of the neighborhood. She seemed to bring sunshine to everyone they met. But whenever people looked at Raine, they took a step back. It seemed that he and Sophie cancelled each other out. For her, people's faces lit up, and for him, they darkened.

But even though everyone smiled at Sophie as she handed out the flyers, some just read them over quickly before letting them fall to the ground. Each time someone tossed one, Raine wanted to stop and shout at them, *don't you care?*

When they were nearly out of flyers, Raine said, "Maybe we should call it a night."

"Really?" she asked. "There's still a ton of places we could hit yet." Then she stopped and sniffed the air. "Rosario's. Have you ever had their chicken and rice?"

"I don't think so."

"Oh, it's this great restaurant that serves authentic Puerto Rican food. My mom grew up in this neighborhood, and she knows the owners. She took me there the other night," Sophie said. "It should still be open, and it's right around the corner. My treat."

"Sure, I guess so," Raine said. "Won't your mother be worried? It's getting late."

"No, it's perfectly fine. She won't worry. She knows I'm helping the church."

Rosario's was a tiny place. The décor was gaudy, and the lighting was dim, but everyone there looked to be having a good time. Raine and Sophie sat next to each other at the counter, each with a huge bowl of chicken and rice. Sophie told him more about her mom's nonprofit organization and how she hoped to follow in her footsteps someday.

When their bellies were full and their bowls cleared, Sophie turned to him and said, "Can I see your face?"

"What?"

"By touching it," she said. "You swooped down to my rescue last night. I know there's something special about you. I just want to see who you are."

Raine hesitated. What if Sophie felt his face and was horrified by him? But somehow, he knew that she wouldn't be. She had gone out of her way to be friends with him.

"Sure. Just promise me you won't freak out."

Sophie held her hands up near him and said, "There's not much that frightens me, Raine."

He took her hands into his and guided them to his face. At first, she laid her hands on his cheeks and kept them there. Her palms were soft and warm. The last time he had felt anyone touch his face was when his mother was alive. As she moved her fingertips over his rough, leathery skin and protruding brows, he watched her face for signs of fright. But there were none. Instead, she looked happy and curious. After nearly ten minutes of mapping his face, she let out a gentle sigh and removed her hands.

"Such pain," she said. "A lifetime, maybe more. But yet so unique. Can you smile for me?"

"Why?"

"I want to see it," she said.

Raine tried, but it came out awkward and forced. Sophie touched his lips, followed their curve up to his cheeks. "I mean a *real* smile. Think about something that makes you happy."

He didn't have to think too hard. He thought of Sophie's red hair bouncing in the morning sunlight as he watched from his perch. The yellow headband. Her icy eyes that saw nothing, even though she seemed to take in everything all at once. But what made him smile the most was just the fact of her touching his face. The fact that she knew exactly what he looked like, and she accepted him. He smiled wide and relaxed beneath her hands.

"That's it," she said. "That's a real smile."

CHAPTER
5

"They say our cities shed too much light pollution," Sophie said, aiming her face up at the night sky. "There will be numerous generations in the future who have no clue what the stars look like anymore. It's sad that so many people who can see, never take the time for the things worth seeing."

They walked down the sidewalk together. She walked without her cane, opting to hook her arm in his and let Raine lead her home. She was right about the stars, Raine thought. He remembered the nights in France. The stars bloomed like flowers in the blackness. He remembered thinking they were billions of eyes looking down on him. He looked above, but only a few twinkles managed to make it through the haze of New York City's light.

"My mother once told me that the spirits of those you loved and lost took to the stars after they died. Each one represented a soul looking back at you," Raine said. "In France, in the countryside, the stars are quite the sight to behold."

"So how long did you live there?" Sophie asked.

They were almost a block from home. He wished they were farther away. "A long time," he said.

"But we're about the same age, and you barely have an accent."

"I mean, a long time ago," Raine said quickly. "I've spent most of my life in Brooklyn."

They approached Sophie's apartment building. Outside, on the front steps, a man and a woman stood talking—maybe arguing. She was wearing jeans, and he was in a business suit. She looked frustrated. He seemed impatient. And oddly familiar.

The man in the suit glanced over and saw the two of them. Then he strode forward, calling out Sophie's name. As he got closer, Raine suddenly recognized him. It was Joseph Waldermann, the developer who wanted to tear down the church. What was he doing here?

"Sophie Arianna Waldermann!" he said sharply. "Where have you been? I was supposed to pick you up hours ago to go to the Aackersons' party."

"I'm sorry," Sophie said. "I forgot."

Raine felt an emptiness in his stomach. A black hole that threatened to collapse. Sophie Waldermann? The truth hit him like a brick to the head, yet Raine still struggled to believe it.

"Joseph Waldermann is your father?" Raine asked Sophie just as Waldermann walked up, pointing at Raine, and said, "I know you, from the church. What are you doing with my daughter?"

Raine didn't know what to say. Anger thumped in his chest. His jaw tightened. His claws began to emerge. But no, he had to control himself. He couldn't let his anger come out now, while he was standing right here in the middle of the neighborhood. Not in front of Sophie. And definitely not in front of Joseph Waldermann.

"It's okay, Dad," Sophie said. "He's a good friend. We were just passing out flyers for the church service."

Waldermann bowed his head and seemed to collect himself. Raine couldn't tell what thoughts were whirling around in his head. But when he looked up at Raine, he smiled. It wasn't a real, heartfelt smile, but a wormy, sly smile.

"My apologies—" he said, waiting for Raine to fill in his name.

"Raine."

"Right, Raine," Waldermann said. "I was just unaware that my daughter was spending time with boys. You can imagine a father's surprise."

"Yeah," Raine said. "I suppose it would hit hard. Like a wrecking ball."

"A wrecking ball?" Sophie asked.

At the mention of the wrecking ball, Waldermann shot him a questioning look.

"Yeah, kind of like the one on the crane parked in front of the church," Raine added, looking from Waldermann to Sophie.

She cocked her head toward her father. "Is that the 'big deal' you've been talking about, Dad? The church?"

Waldermann tried to suppress a satisfied grin. "It's just good business, sweetheart. Imagine that old church gone and luxury condos in its place."

"Luxury condos. In this neighborhood?" Sophie questioned.

"Everywhere in Brooklyn is hip now," Waldermann said. "You know how many people with real money want to live here, just so they can say they do? And when they all move in, they're going to need nice places to eat and shop."

"And let me guess," Sophie said. "You have plans for 'developing' all the other properties around here, too?"

Waldermann smiled. "That's what I do. Improve neighborhoods."

"There are good people here," Sophie said. "Good people who will lose their homes, their community."

"That's progress, sweetheart. Survival of the fittest."

"More like survival of the richest," Sophie corrected him. She took out her cane and began to walk toward her apartment building.

"She can be dramatic at times," Waldermann said to Raine.

As soon as she heard that, Sophie swung around and walked over to Raine. She found his face with her hands, then reached up and kissed him on the cheek.

"I had a wonderful night, really."

Raine was too stunned to say anything.

Sophie turned back again, tapping her cane hard on the pavement as she moved past her father. She whacked her cane hard against his shin.

"Time to go, Dad."

Waldermann ran after his daughter, but Sophie's mother stepped in the way.

"You can forget about taking Sophie tonight. It's late, and you've upset her. The way you talked to her, and that boy, the first real friend she's made here. It's just insensitive, Joseph. I'll drive her to your place in the morning."

Raine felt his body relax. He hadn't realized how tense he had gotten talking to Waldermann. But he still felt he scored a victory—a small one, at least. That probably had something to do with Sophie. No girl had ever kissed him before.

Raine quickly walked across the street with a smile on his face even though he saw that the wrecking ball had been reattached to the crane. He went inside the church and to the pastor's quarters. Over the years, he had never bothered any of the pastors while they slept. As their steward, he felt it was awkward to ever wake them for anything—no matter how big or small the situation. But this time he was compelled to knock.

After a moment, Pastor Hernandez opened the door and looked at him sleepily.

"I'm sorry, Pastor. I shouldn't have bothered you—I'll let you get some sleep."

The pastor waved off the apology. "No, no, never mind. Please, what do you need?"

"It's Sophie."

The pastor stood up straighter, more attentive. "Is she all right?"

"Yes," Raine said. "She's fine. But it's just something I found out about her. Her father is Joseph Waldermann."

"Oh my," the pastor said. "She's so unlike him."

Raine nodded. "And I found out more bad news."

"Yes?"

Raine told the pastor everything Waldermann was planning. The condos. The shops. The restaurants. It wasn't just the church that would be affected. Waldermann planned on changing the entire neighborhood.

"How can we stop that?" Raine asked.

"I don't know if we can," the pastor said. He rubbed his hand over his head. "But I'll talk to the church board first thing in the morning. Owen might consider backing out of the deal."

But Raine decided on a different plan.

After the pastor went back to sleep, Raine darted up to his room. He took off his human clothes and put the loincloth he wore during the day back on. From his ledge, he spied Waldermann outside of Sophie's apartment. He was just getting into his limousine. He and Sophie's mother must have continued their argument for a while after Raine had left.

When the car sped forward, Raine took to the air and followed it. With each stroke of his powerful wings, the anger swelled inside him. His heart chugged loudly in his chest. He bared his massive fangs and unsheathed his claws. His head grew hot in anger. The angrier he got, the more grotesque and frightening Raine's face became. He felt more like a beast than a man.

When the limousine stopped at a traffic light, Raine broke into a dive. In his first swoop over the car, he tore off the roof. Waldermann and his driver screamed in surprise. On his second pass, Raine plucked the driver out of his seat and flung him into the alley, where he landed in a pile of garbage. On the third pass, Raine came down with all his power on the hood of the car, flattening it with a thunderous crash. Raine looked up to see Waldermann cowering in fear. The businessman scrambled out of his seat and onto the trunk of the car.

"Don't hurt me!" Waldermann pleaded.

Raine walked across the destroyed car as he approached Waldermann. Each footstep crunched metal and glass. He made each step louder and more terrifying. He reached down and lifted Waldermann up by the collar of his shirt.

"The church is not yours to take," he warned.

As quickly as he had swooped down on the car, Raine released Waldermann and rose upward into the darkness.

CHAPTER
6

The next morning, before sunrise, Pastor Hernandez got dressed. In the small kitchen, he turned on the coffee maker. While the coffee brewed, he retrieved the morning paper and sat down to read. Plastered all over the front page was a grainy traffic camera photo of what looked like a monster standing on the wreckage of a limousine.

"Raine!" he shouted up to the bell tower.

Raine climbed down and stepped into the kitchen. "I know, I know. I shouldn't have."

The pastor held up the newspaper. "What will people think happened here?"

"I'm sorry. I wasn't thinking. I just needed to do something. Anything."

"That poor man must have been frightened to death. I told you to be patient. It will all work out."

Raine looked at the ground. "It's just . . . nothing else is working. No one cares enough about the church to save it, so I thought I could scare Waldermann away."

"Well, it looks like you left quite the impression," the pastor said. "I hope for our sake no one recognized you. Especially Waldermann."

"He doesn't know."

"How can you be sure?"

Raine paused. "My appearance can reflect my emotions. As angry as I was, I'm sure I looked far from human."

"Well, I'm going to talk to Owen, anyway," the pastor said. "Maybe he'll change his mind if he knows what Waldermann plans to do."

After Pastor Hernandez left, Raine made his way to his room. He sat behind his small desk and wrote about his time spent with Sophie. He wondered how much longer he'd be able to record his days. He had been around for three hundred years. He hadn't thought about death since the cathedral was moved to Brooklyn. He had no reason to. But ever since he had woken up to that wrecking ball, it was on his mind, constantly. Maybe it was for the best. Maybe he had served his purpose in this world.

He took off his human clothes, put on his gargoyle loincloth, and climbed out onto the ledge of the bell tower. Crouched down and overlooking the street, he took a deep breath and exhaled as the sun rose, and his body turned slowly to stone. He was weary and tired, but he fought it. On the brink of falling asleep, he heard a noise. The front doors of the church creaked open.

His instinct was to swoop down and investigate, but he couldn't move. He could only listen.

The front doors swung shut. He heard footsteps in the sanctuary below.

"Pastor Hernandez?" a voice called. "Raine?"

He thought he knew the voice, but couldn't quite place it. Whoever it was, they didn't call out too loudly or really seem interested in finding someone.

The footsteps moved down the stairs and into the kitchen. After some shuffling around, the pantry door opened. The intruder climbed the ladder. Opened the trapdoor to Raine's room with a thud. From the sounds of it, the intruder was rummaging through Raine's things. His remaining drawings. His clothes. His . . .

Raine realized in horror that his latest journal sat on his desk. In the open. His entire life—exposed. Raine tried moving his arms, his wings, his legs. He had to break free. He had to stop whoever it was before he found the journal. But Raine couldn't. He was cursed to his stone form.

"What's this?" the intruder said.

In that instant, Raine placed the voice: Joseph Waldermann. Raine could hear him flipping through the pages of his journal. He imagined Waldermann reading his final passages. Uncovering all his secrets. His life. His feelings for Sophie.

After a few minutes, Waldermann spoke into his phone, "Send Terence to my office." He hung up and then muttered, "This boy won't be spending any more time with my daughter."

Raine heard Waldermann climb down the ladder and eventually leave the church. He listened for hours, in case Waldermann came back. But he didn't. Raine did his best to stay awake, but after a few hours, he grew too tired and fell asleep.

✦ ✦ ✦ ✦ ✦

After a long, rough day with little sleep, the sun set and released Raine. His body slowly unlocked. Stone softened to flesh and blood. His heart awoke and began pumping. His lungs inflated. His eyes opened. When the last sliver of sun disappeared under the horizon, Raine lurched upward in a great yawn. He shook his entire body, then arched his back until the ligaments and bones relaxed. He exhaled deeply.

"I figured it out the other night, you know," Sophie said.

Raine turned with a start. There sat Sophie on the ledge next to him. Her legs dangled over the side. He was taken aback for a moment, because she sat in the exact same spot as she had in his dream days ago.

"How'd you get up here? It isn't safe. You could fall."

"I may be blind, Raine, but I'm not incapable," she said. "Besides, if I fell, you'd catch me, right?"

Raine nodded, but after realizing she couldn't see him, he said, "Yes. I'd try." She had figured out his secret. "So what gave me away?"

She still hadn't looked in his direction. Her icy eyes stared off at the city skyline.

"That night you saved me, I knew you were special. Not because you took care of those guys, but when you left, I didn't hear any footsteps as you ran off. Just a powerful gust of air. The sound of wings."

"You knew then?" Raine asked.

Finally, she turned in his direction. Those icy eyes. The red hair tucked behind her ears and flowing to her shoulders. The same yellow headband.

"Not completely," she said. "I did some research. Came up with some theories and remembered you talking about the grotesques."

"So now you know that I'm a monster."

"No, no, no," Sophie said. "Not a monster. Not at all. You're a work of art. Unique. And important to me."

She scooted closer to Raine and took his hands into hers. Then, to his surprise, she leaning over and kissed him. Raine wrapped his arms, and then his wings, around her—and kissed her back. Never had he been that close to anyone before, besides his mother. As Sophie kissed him, he felt an energy between them. A humming, vibrating warmth that spread outward from him and into her. He remembered the stories his mother had told him. Fairy tales.

A princess kissing a frog.

Beauty and the Beast.

He half-expected to feel a transformation come over him. His curse expelled from his body. But when she broke away from him, his wings remained. His tail. His gnarled face and leathery skin. He tried to curb his disappointment. Maybe she was doing all this to simply get back at her father. To cause him harm. But he shook his doubts away. He didn't want to ruin the moment.

Sophie opened her eyes and looked at his face. Again, her icy stare seemed to penetrate him, go through him. "So. You can fly."

Raine nodded. "Yes, I can."

"I bet it's amaz—"

Before she could finish her question, Raine wrapped her in his arms and launched into the night sky.

CHAPTER
7

Raine carried Sophie over the city.
They flew over the Empire State Building, the
Chrysler Building, the Brooklyn Bridge, Coney
Island, and the Statue of Liberty. At each
landmark he whispered into her ear his best
descriptions of them. He told her about the lights
of the city, how they glittered like a million stars.
When the air grew a bit chilly, he swung around
and headed home.

Raine gently swooped down to the bell
tower and carried Sophie inside.

"That was magical!" Sophie said. "The
wind in my hair—the thrill of the dives—it was
like being weightless." Raine set her down and
she stepped away, but turned back to him and
kissed him again. "Thank you."

"Listen," Raine said. "There's something you need to know. My uniqueness. It comes with a curse as well."

"How so?"

Raine stepped to his desk and shifted the papers around, trying to make his room look more organized. "Each living grotesque is born from the transference of a life force. Stone by day, flesh and blood at night. Each life force is bound to a significant landmark or building. I am bound to the Cathedral of Pas-de-Calais, France. The same stone and brick brought here to erect St. Genevieve's."

"To this church?"

"Yes."

"So if the church is destroyed?"

"I die."

"What? How? If the cathedral in France was destroyed and moved here, why didn't that kill you?"

"It's more than stone and mortar, Sophie. It's the significance. It's energy. Purpose."

"Like a soul?"

"Some would say that, yes," Raine said. "But that's not the biggest problem."

"There's more?" Sophie asked.

"Your father stopped by today," Raine said. "I think he was looking for me, but, well, it was daytime, so he didn't find me. But he found my room. My things. He took my journal, Sophie. He'll learn what I am."

Sophie thought about it. "No one will ever believe him, whatever he says about you."

"But that's not the real problem," Raine said.

"Don't worry, Raine. I'll talk to my dad. I'll get him to change his mind."

"I just feel helpless," Raine said. "I'm supposed to protect this building, and I can't."

"It's not over yet," Sophie said, kissing him good-bye.

Sophie carefully stepped to the trapdoor, feeling its outline with her feet. She bent down and opened it up, then felt for the ladder with her hands.

"I can fly you home," Raine suggested.

Sophie looked up and smiled at him. "Please, Raine. I climbed up here. I can find my way back down. But you can take me flying again another time."

And like that, she ducked beneath the trapdoor and was gone. Raine went to the ledge and listened to her cane tap-tap-tapping across the street. He watched over her until she was safely inside her apartment building.

Raine put on his hoodie, and he, too, climbed downstairs. He found Pastor Hernandez sitting in the kitchen in his pajamas. A plate of shortbread cookies and a small glass of milk sat in front of him.

"Sophie brought them," he told Raine. "They're really good."

Raine sat down across from the pastor and picked up a cookie. "You can't sleep? That can't mean good news."

"I did my best, Raine," the pastor said. "But the purchase agreement has been signed. It's out of our hands now. We have this weekend's service. Then we're done."

Raine felt queasy. Now it would only be a matter of days until he was no more. Three hundred years had come to this. To his impending death. His failure.

"Sophie's our only hope," Raine said. "Only she can stop her father."

"It appears that way."

Raine heard the church doors swing open. He dashed upstairs, expecting Sophie. The pastor followed him.

"Did you forget something?" Raine asked.

"No," a deep voice replied.

A large man stood in the middle of the sanctuary. He wore a leather coat and stocking hat. He looked like a professional wrestler. Raine knew he wasn't there for the pastor.

"The new owner wants you out," the man said.

The pastor stepped forward and said, "The purchase agreement says we have another week. Until then, we're staying."

"Not you," the man said to the pastor. Then he pointed at Raine. "Him. He has to go."

"He's my steward," the pastor said. "He stays here with me."

The large man shoved the pastor out of the way.

Raine leaped forward, grabbing the man by the front of his shirt, and looked into his face.

"You really don't want to start this, do you?" he demanded.

The large man shoved Raine backward.

"Time for you to go," he said.

Raine's heart raced. His muscles tensed. The anger inside him frothed, looking for a way out.

"I'm not leaving!" Raine shouted.

With a fury he unfolded his wings, and they ripped out of his hoodie. There he stood in the dim sanctuary, his massive wings outstretched. The intruder wiped his mouth. He didn't show any fear on his face, but Raine could smell it. It dripped out of him in his sweat.

"Raine! Don't!" the pastor yelled.

The men lurched toward one another, fists up, ready to fight. But Raine easily overpowered the intruder. After the man landed a punch square on Raine's jaw, Raine spun around quickly. Then he grabbed the man by the back of his coat and took flight, crashing through the roof of the church.

Up and up he flew. His powerful wings pumped the air and shot them skyward. Each stroke brought them higher above the city. The intruder screamed and flailed as he saw the city shrinking beneath them.

"I wouldn't wiggle around too much. I don't know how much longer your coat will hold you," Raine warned.

"I was just supposed to scare you! To keep you away from the girl!"

At the pinnacle of their flight, Raine yanked the man closer to his grotesque face.

"Look at me! Look at me!" Raine yelled. "Do you think I can be frightened?"

The man broke down. "Don't kill me. Don't kill me."

"I'm not going to kill you," Raine said. "I need you to do something for me."

"Anything," the man said. "Anything!"

"Tell Waldermann to cancel the deal," Raine said. "The church doesn't belong to him."

Raine flipped backward and rocketed back down to the church.

CHAPTER
8

At five in the morning, Raine knelt atop the church, repairing the hole he had made earlier when he blasted through the roof. When he was done, he sat down and watched the city below him. A newspaper delivery truck rattled through the streets below. A police car cruised slowly by, but then sped away with lights and siren on. Above, a jet streaked across the night sky.

He wondered if he had made things worse. Would Waldermann send more hired muscle? Would he call the police? Send a SWAT team? The National Guard? A crane was one thing, but against rifles and machine guns, he didn't stand a chance. Or maybe Sophie was right. No one would believe that one of the grotesques

up on St. Genevieve's was behind the attack
on Waldermann's limo. The one thing Raine
had learned in America was that people were
fascinated by outlandish tales, but they rarely
believed them.

Raine got down from the roof and put
his tools away in the shed. When he came back
to the front of the church, he heard Sophie
approaching, tapping her cane on the sidewalk.
After all that had happened, he was overjoyed
to see her. The red hair. The yellow headband.
Those icy blue eyes. He met her halfway and
said, "I'm so glad to see you."

But she shook her head.

"What?" Raine asked. What's wrong?"

Sophie broke down in tears. "Dad said no.
I begged and pleaded, but he just said I was too
young to understand. I hate him."

Raine took her into his arms and hugged
her. "Don't say that, Sophie. Hate is such a vile
thing, and he's your father no matter what."

"But he's going to kill you!"

Raine shook his head. "No, he's not. He's
just taking the church."

"But that's the same thing!"

"Just don't worry about me," he said.

"I'm staying here with you, no matter what he tries to do."

Raine wanted nothing more. "It's almost morning," he said.

Together they entered the church and went to the pantry. They climbed up to his room, and he changed into his daytime loincloth.

"I have to go out to the ledge now," he told her.

"I'm coming with you."

"It's too dangerous," Raine said.

"I don't care," she said. "If you leave me here, I'll just climb out myself. I'll be fine."

Raine saw that she meant it. He looked at her and saw her strength. Never in three hundred years did he ever think he could be in love. But just days before his demise, he was happy to find it. Lucky even.

"Okay," he said.

He lifted her up in his arms and carefully climbed out onto his ledge. He set her down.

"It's almost time."

She leaned up on her tiptoes and kissed him again.

"I'll be right by your side."

Raine smiled. Then he turned away and took his place on the ledge. He crouched down as the sun broke across the horizon. Raine's strength withdrew. His bones locked in petrification. His muscles froze into place, and his skin hardened to stone.

Sophie sat next to the grotesque and leaned into his side. Her eyes grew droopy, weary. She tried her best to stay awake, but after a while she, too, fell asleep.

✦ ✦ ✦ ✦ ✦

Sophie dreamed of France, the cathedral, and Raine with his curse lifted.

Raine dreamed of France, the cathedral, and Sophie with her eyesight.

Both awoke at the sound of the voice, but only Sophie could move.

"Sophie!" Mr. Waldermann said. "What are *you* doing out here?"

Groggy, Sophie carefully sat up and turned in the direction of her father's voice.

"Dad? I could ask you the same."

Out of the corner of his eye, Raine saw Waldermann, dressed in jeans and a polo shirt. He held a sledgehammer in his hands. It was so new it still had the price tag on its handle. Even though Sophie couldn't see the hammer, he swung it around behind him to hide it.

"This is my property, sweetheart. I have a right to be here."

Sophie stood on shaky legs. "I know you took Raine's journal. I know you know the truth about him."

"Well," Waldermann began. "After your *friend* scared off Terence—and no one scares Terence—I decided to read a little more of his journal. So yes, I do know the truth. He's the monster that attacked me the other night."

"And that's why you're up here right now—during the day!"

Waldermann looked below. On the street, a few people took notice of the figures standing up on the ledge. One of them pointed.

"Sophie," Mr. Waldermann said. "Listen. It's not safe up here. Let me help you inside. We can talk about it there."

"Talk about it? Now? I talked to you about it last night, and you wouldn't listen."

Waldermann looked down again. More and more people from the neighborhood had gathered.

"I just want you to be safe, honey."

"Don't 'honey' me!" Sophie protested. "Why don't you tell them?" She gestured to where she thought the street was below them. Where bystanders now stood in a larger group. "Tell them your plans! How the church is only the first step. How you want to destroy their neighborhood."

Raine listened with glee. Sophie was brilliant. She knew she had an audience below and was taking the opportunity to divulge her father's plans.

Waldermann held up his hand to her. "Calm down, Sophie!"

"I will not calm down!"

"I just want the best for you," he said. "A better life."

"A better life?" Sophie said. "I live in the neighborhood you want to destroy."

"Are you out to save this church?" Waldermann yelled back, finally losing it. "Or are you more interested in saving that *thing*—that monster you've been sneaking around with?" He took a quick look below. The crowd continued to grow.

"That's it, isn't it? You're not here for me. You're here for *him*," Sophie said. "That's why you brought a sledgehammer. To destroy him!"

Waldermann was shocked. "How did you—"

"I can hear its metal head grinding the stone of the ledge behind you." Sophie said.

Waldermann stepped forward. "Enough! This is over. Step aside, Sophie."

"No!" Sophie cried. She went to stand between her father and Raine. But she misjudged her step. She lost her balance.

Frozen, petrified, Raine watched it all happen. The last three hundred years seemed to

have gone faster than the three seconds it took
for Sophie to plummet to the ground below.
Raine wanted to reach out, dive, soar to her
rescue, catch her before she hit the ground, but
he couldn't. He could only watch.

On the street in front of the church, the
neighbors gasped. Some even screamed as
Sophie fell. Waldermann knelt at the edge
of the church and looked below, horrified.
Crying. Weeping for his only child. At that
moment, Raine felt sorry for him. All that
time, he had grown to hate the man. But Raine
understood loss.

Waldermann rushed down the tower. On
the grounds, both he and the pastor ran out to
Sophie. Raine watched from overhead as the
neighbors rushed to Sophie's aid. Moments
later the police arrived. Then an ambulance.
The whole tragedy replayed in his mind the rest
of the day. He couldn't sleep. Couldn't think
about anything else. The loss of the church. His
impending demise.

It all felt so trivial.

CHAPTER
9

That night, as the sun set, Raine awoke from his stony slumber. He couldn't remember falling asleep. But when the warmth sped back into his body, and he opened his eyes, he didn't see the indigo of night, but a great circle of light below—a ring of candles around where Sophie had fallen.

Raine climbed into his room. Changed into his sneakers, baggy jeans, and hoodie. He clambered down the pantry ladder and dashed through the kitchen. He burst out of the church doors and ran into the street.

A mass of people formed a ring around the church lot. They held hands and sang and prayed. People from all over the neighborhood had laid flowers against the fence. Candles flickered in the night breeze. Children had painted posters and hung them on the fence. He read them all.

Be Strong!

Have faith.

You are in our hearts.

In our prayers.

We love you!

Paper lanterns. Balloons. Stuffed bears. Everywhere he looked, he saw gifts from people in the neighborhood. Raine hadn't realized, until now, how many people Sophie had touched.

Under his hood, Raine did his best not to cry. He made his way through the crowd. When he was almost a block away from the church, a hand grabbed his shoulder.

Pastor Hernandez reached out and hugged him. "I'm so sorry, Raine. I'm so sorry."

Raine hugged him back. "Is she—gone?"

The pastor shook his head. "No. But the prognosis isn't good."

"I have to see her."

The pastor held onto Raine tighter. "Don't do that to yourself."

"She's dying because of me."

"No, it was an accident."

"You don't understand," Raine told him. "She was up there to protect me. Waldermann brought a sledgehammer." Raine paused. Wiped a tear from his cheek. "I'm only standing here because she stopped him."

The pastor hugged him again and said, "Then go."

Raine ran into a dark alley. He removed his hoodie and took to the air. In the past when he was upset, flying over the city made him feel better. But all he was interested in now was getting to the hospital to see Sophie one last time.

He landed on the roof of the hospital and put his hoodie back on. Inside, he asked at the nurse's station for Sophie's room. When he got to the room, he stepped in and saw her. Her face was cut and bruised. Her head had been shaved, and she had a large white bandage wrapped around it. They had her hooked up to a ventilator and numerous machines that quietly beeped. Her mother sat in a chair and stared hopelessly at Sophie.

Raine went to the foot of her bed and stood in silence as he stared at her. She looked so broken. She had a cast on her arm and another on one of her legs.

"You're Raine, Sophie's friend?" her mother asked.

Raine nodded. "I'm sorry. I had to see her."

Sophie's mother stood up and walked over to him. He was afraid she would ask him to leave, but instead she leaned into him and hugged him. She started to cry.

"They had to cut a piece out of her skull to relieve the swelling in her brain," she said. "They don't think she'll make it through the night. I'm so scared."

"I'm sorry, Mrs. Waldermann," Raine said. "I'm so sorry."

"She really cared about you, you know," she said. She stepped back and dabbed her eyes with a tissue. "With the divorce and everything with her father, she needed someone. I think with you and the church, she had really found something to believe in. You were able to give her a tiny bit of happiness during a rough time for us. So please don't be sorry. I'm thankful."

"Can I stay with her for a bit?" Raine asked.

"Yes," she said. "Please."

Raine scooted a chair up to Sophie's bed and then sat. He leaned over Sophie and kissed her forehead. Then he reached in and took her hand in his. Before she had been so warm, tender. But in that bed, her skin felt cold. As though her life were pulling away from her body.

Sitting there with Sophie's hand in his, he thought about the last few days. She had brought him happiness, too. Probably more than he had felt in the past three hundred years.

Sitting there, looking at this girl he had come to love, he remembered the three rules to his curse. One of them, he no longer felt was a curse but a gift. The same gift his mother had given him so long ago.

One life to give, to make it right.

Raine took a deep breath and stood up. He leaned over and kissed Sophie's cheek, then her hand. He walked around the bed and hugged her mother again.

"Take good care of her, okay?"

Sophie's mother nodded. Dabbed her eyes with her tissue again. "When she wakes up, she'll want to see you."

"She'll know exactly where to find me."

Raine walked out of the room, up the stairs, and then onto the roof. Out in the night breeze, he took a deep breath and pulled off his hoodie. With a great stroke of his wings, he launched himself into the air. He flew over the whole city again. Past the Chrysler Building. He swooped around the spire of the Empire State Building. Over Coney Island and Yankee Stadium. He still missed the sights of France, but New York City at night held a special place in his heart as well. His tour complete, he arched toward St. Genevieve's. He had never seen so many people in the neighborhood before. The street outside the church was jammed. Their songs and prayers hummed overhead. And the flickers of a thousand candles reflected in his eyes.

When he climbed into his room in the bell tower to change, he noticed Pastor Hernandez waiting for him.

"How's she doing?" the pastor asked.

"Not good," Raine said. "I'm afraid she won't make it through the night."

"I'm sorry, Raine. She was such a spirited girl."

Raine bowed his head, then looked up at his dear friend.

"There are a lot of voices outside. A lot of people looking for hope."

"I'm having a special midnight service," the pastor said. "I was hoping you could join us."

Raine took another deep breath. "I'd love to. But I have to do something important first."

Pastor Hernandez bowed his head slowly, then extended his hand and shook Raine's. "I understand."

Raine pulled the pastor to him and hugged him. "Thank you for everything. Take care of this church for me, okay?"

The pastor nodded. After he left, Raine changed into his loincloth. He climbed out of the bell tower and took his position on the ledge. Crouching in his spot, he closed his eyes and searched inward. Deep inside he knew there was sparkling light—his life force. Using every ounce of strength he had, he summoned it up and out of his mouth. He filled his thoughts with Sophie, focused on her lying in her hospital bed. Then, the spark flew across the city. As it flew, he felt the life leave him. Slowly, bit by bit, he was turning back into stone. First his bones. Then his muscles and ligaments. Until even his skin hardened into stone. And in that moment, Raine was no more.

CHAPTER
10

Pastor Hernandez had never seen St. Genevieve's so full. The neighborhood had crammed inside the small sanctuary. Every seat was taken. People even stood at the back of the church. Candles flickered in everyone's hands. He stood at the front of the church. Nervous.

"Hope," he began. "When I first came here to St. Genevieve's, I saw a lot of people without hope. And in today's world, with its politics, its crime, wars raging overseas, and pollution clouding our skies, I realize that hope is a difficult thing to hold onto."

The pastor paused and gestured around to the full church. "But look around you. Whether you think so or not, hope has power. It can change things. It can brighten our lives."

Pastor Hernandez rubbed his neck. "Today, we witnessed something horrific. And right now, Sophie Waldermann clings to life. The doctors say she won't last the night. My hope is that we won't forget her no matter what happens. She hasn't lived in this neighborhood for as long as many of us. But the fact that you're here is proof she has had an impact on your lives."

The pastor bowed his head. "Now let us pray."

The whole congregation went silent as the pastor began his prayer.

Midway through, that silence was broken as the doors to the sanctuary creaked open. People toward the back turned around to see who had entered, and their gasps of amazement drew more eyes.

The pastor looked up, and then quickly ran down the aisle to meet Sophie as she limped her way forward. She was still dressed in her hospital gown. Her casts had been removed, and her shaved hair had started to grow back. Scars had already formed where skin had been stitched together. And atop her head, amid her rapidly growing hair, was her yellow headband. People reached out to her as the pastor gave her a huge hug.

"You don't seem as amazed to see me as everyone else," Sophie said.

The pastor shook his head. "I knew you'd need to return."

Sophie took a deep breath and looked at the pastor. "I need to see him."

The pastor nodded. "Of course. Here, I'll help you."

Sophie shook her head. "Thanks, but I don't need it." She gestured to her body with her hands. "Everything is healing. I've even regained my sight."

They left the sanctuary and made their way through the kitchen, then into the pantry. Before climbing the ladder into Raine's room, Sophie turned back to the pastor.

"Once we explain to my father what happened—Raine's sacrifice and what that means," Sophie said, "the church and this neighborhood will be saved."

Pastor Hernandez looked down at his feet. "Raine isn't the only one who's made a sacrifice tonight."

"I know," Sophie said as she climbed up to Raine's room.

She looked at his things: the newspaper clippings, the small statuette of Lady Liberty, the stuffed bear from Coney Island, charcoal sketches of people taking a night stroll in Central Park, and the easel with a watercolor of the Brooklyn Bridge at night—now finished.

Carefully, she climbed out of the bell tower and out onto the ledge. Adjusting to her newfound sight, she looked over the entire neighborhood. The candles. The buildings. The people. It all amazed her. She found Raine crouched motionless on the ledge. She ran her hands over the stone of his back and shoulders.

At the hospital, when she awoke, she couldn't explain it, but she was compelled to return to the church. She felt bound to this building. She had to protect it.

Then she understood what Raine had done.

Tired, she sat next to Raine and leaned into him. Her hospital gown grew tight along her back. Beneath the fabric something writhed to be free. Then after growing fully, her wings ripped through the back of the gown and unfurled. White, feathered. Like the wings of a dove. They flapped briefly in their newfound freedom, then tucked around her for warmth.

She dangled her legs over the edge and waited all night for the sunrise.

It didn't disappoint.

SCOTT R. WELVAERT

GROTESQUE

SCOTT R. WELVAERT

About the Author

Scott Welvaert has published numerous titles, including two other books in the Tartan House series, *The 13th Floor* and *The Alabaster Ring*, and two middle grade fantasy adventure novels, *The Curse of the Wendigo* and *The Mosquito King*. His book of poetry, *Pacific*, won the Sol Books Award and was subsequently published through Skywater Publishing. He graduated with an M.F.A. in Creative Writing and currently lives in Minnesota with his wife, two daughters, and a dog named Sparrow.

Questions to Think About

1. Both Raine and Sophie are unique individuals. They have traits that some people might see as disabilities, but those traits are also part of what makes them special. What makes you unique? Do have any talents or abilities that you are proud of? They could be as simple as being able to wiggle your ears or as difficult as being able to juggle.

2. A "cause" is a goal or interest that a person or group of people fight for. Raine and Sophie have a common cause; they both struggle to help save the church and the neighborhood around it. What sort of causes do you believe in? How can you help support these causes?

3. Imagine what it would be like if you had wings like Raine and could fly. He likes to soar above the city. How would you use this ability? Are there things you would do or places you would go see?

THE 13TH FLOOR

Sam is happy to be included with the popular football players, who happen to play the same video game he does. When they get their hands on a pirated copy of *The 13th Floor*, a game banned for violence and gore, Sam gives it a try. Soon he and his friends find the game to be so hypnotic that they can't stop playing, even after it begins to take control of their real lives.

THE ALABASTER RING

When Ethan receives a box of his dad's old belongings, what he finds puts him at odds with a killer from an international crime organization. Will Ethan and his new friend, Kendra, find what they are looking for before they come face to face with a criminal mastermind?

DEEP WATER HOTEL

Michael suffers from a mysterious and painful lung disease. But he's thrilled when his favorite online celebrity raises the funds to grant his last wish—to visit the world's only deep-water hotel. Submerged miles below the water's surface, Michael discovers horrifying sea creatures, and a shocking secret is revealed.

READ MORE FROM 12-STORY LIBRARY

Every 12-Story Library book is available in many formats, including Amazon Kindle and Apple iBooks. For more information, visit your device's store or 12StoryLibrary.com.